Story
for a
Black
Night

OTHER GRAPHIA TITLES

CHECK OUT GRAPHIABOOKS.COM

Story for a Black Night

Clayton Bess

GRAPHIA

AN IMPRINT OF HOUGHTON MIFFLIN COMPANY BOSTON

www.graphiabooks.com

Graphia and the Graphia logo are trademarks
of Houghton Mifflin Company.

The text of this book is set in Stempel Garamond.

Library of Congress Cataloging-in-Publication Data

Bess, Clayton.
Story for a black night / by Clayton Bess.
p. cm.
Summary: An African father tells his son about the disaster
that followed the night a baby with smallpox was abandoned
in his family's house.

ISBN 0-618-49483-9

[1. Africa— Fiction. 2. Smallpox— Fiction. 3. Family life— Fiction]
I. Title.
PZ7.B4654St
[Fic] 81-13396
AACR2

ISBN-13: 978-0-618-49483-5

Manufactured in the United States of America
WOZ 10 9 8 7 6 5 4 3 2 1

Story
for a
Black
Night

AIN'T THE NIGHT IS BLACK TONIGHT? You children would like to run playing, ain't it? But the darkness be too great for you. By force of storm, electric current came to fail, and tonight people must go back to kerosene, and you must sit with me. And watch sharp. And listen. See the people walk by with their lamps, and see the gold light, how it can bounce and throw their shadows twisting among us, so that smallboys like this one get scary.

"Is there evil tonight, Pa?" Smallboy asks. Is evil here, he wants to know.

Well, we are changing fast, with all of Africa,

but we can't lose evil. Now we have much progress, very much new medicine, very many new cars, and electric current too, that which we lost tonight because it can't stand God.

And they say now that the pox is gone forever. No more smallpox in all the world, no more need for children like you to go for injection, so they now say. We'll see. Take time. We'll see.

Smallboy here wants to know about evil. Let me tell all you children about that. And let me tell you about good. It's heart. It's people and what they do. It's heart. That's evil and that's good and that's all there is.

And don't tell me what preacher says, because he be only one man who don't know more than this man you're talking to. So don't bring me preacher. If he wants to believe that white-man stuff, let him stay there, but I'm talking you now what I know, what I've seen. It's heart.

Let me tell you about Maima Kiawu. I never told you this, ain't it? Hey, you! Smallboy, you! Ain't I never told you about Maima Kiawu?

It was on one night black like this that Maima Kiawu came to us and brought her evil into our house. I was smallboy then, just about like this one, for true. But around here it was different those days. Kakata was smalltown then, and this house where it stands was bush all around, because town had not yet grown to meet us. Now with the coal-tar road, it be like we are part of Kakata, but in those days it was long walk down bad footroad to reach in town. And all around us, it was clean like God put it down. My own pa had cut down the trees and cleared away small circle in the bush, leaving the red ground bare to discourage snake. Middle of circle our house stood lonely.

The day of the night Maima Kiawu brought us her evil, I remember sitting outside by the cookfire watching the last of day. With me watching were Ma, nursing my sister Meatta, and Old Ma, only we four. Pa was dead by this time, killed by snake in the last dry season, by snake they call Old Two-Step. After he was bit, Pa walked only two more steps.

We had just finished eating supper this night when Old Ma whispered to me, clutching my arm, "Momo! Stay close! Leopard near-o!"

How Old Ma could know such thing was always mystery to me. She was blind. Even be it so, she saw many things without her eyes that I could never see even with my own two.

But this night I did see. There at the edge of bush sat leopard, watching me, eyes yellow and pale as the flame in that dying lamp there.

Ma sat like stone with Meatta in her arms. Leopard like wood carving, not moving. Me with my heart in my mouth, chewing it. Old Ma's bone fingers digging my arm.

"It be sign!" Hiss from Old Ma.

I knew she was right. Leopard never so bold as to come near people so. Evil coming-o!

As we watched, leopard twisted his cat head up at the sky and gave long, high cry, that which stopped my blood in my veins. Then without more sound he slid through the trees like shadow on quiet wind, and was gone. Empty bush looked back at me. Bird above stopped singing.

You children don't know how bird sounded here then, but in these thirty years I have not forgotten, unless smallboy of ten hears different from man of forty, that which I don't know. Now bird is gone just as leopard is gone, following deer and monkey since people came to be too plenty. Now maybe once in four months you will see hunter walking coal-tar with red deer meat, but he will want plenty money for it. Or sometime you will find dry monkey hand in the market in Kakata, but it will be too dear and you must buy the fish and leave the monkey. I too sorry for this because red deer meat and monkey meat be sweet.

Hey, Smallboy, ain't you can remember monkey that one time, how sweet? It be longtime, ain't it?

Yes, bird is gone now because the big trees are gone now, with only the rubber bush remaining. Maybe bird can't like sitting in row. Maybe too, sound of cars and trucks passing so near on the coal-tar have frightened bird away. Damn the coal-tar.

But once all the noise here was the sound of bird singing and monkey barking and sometime leopard far away crying, and wind in tall trees. That is why that evening as I listened to silence in the bush, I was scary.

Night was coming to be dark now. Trees around us were so high they blocked the last of sun's light and it was dark of moon. I looked

around at Ma and Old Ma to see them scary too
of leopard coming to weep at our house. Even
Meatta quit from nursing and left the breast
quiet to turn her eyes out to the bush and watch
and listen.

Old Ma had warned me many times of things
too deadly which move in the night, especially
near the water like here. She told me of Mommy
Water, half-woman half-fish, who carries baby
into the river and takes them down to her home
to be her slave or eat them. Old Ma said where
she once lived on the coast, she saw it happen
many times that Mommy Water came and carried baby even off its mother's own back, self.

We sat together now as cookfire died. The
shadows grew fast, dark and long. Too soon it
was deep black night, and if even white man was
there with us, we could not see even him.

"Ma," I said, and my voice came weak inside
me. "Come, let's go in."

"Yes, Momo. All right." My ma's voice was always soft and warm in my ear.

I ran inside and Ma followed, carrying Meatta, and last came Old Ma, who shut the door and locked it and went to each window and closed and locked the shutters to keep out night spirits. All about was black night, but Old Ma, because she had no eyes, moved in darkness as she moved in daylight, always somehow sure where to put hand and foot.

I went to my mat on the floor and lay down, but sleep and me could not pull. I started thinking on that bad-lucky leopard, wondering what trouble he was bringing to our house.

Silence all around.

Ruff-ruff—that Ma, turning over on her mat. *Ruff-ruff*—that Old Ma too. *Urb*—that Meatta in her baby noise. Then suddenly . . .

Kpa! Kpa! Kpa!

First time in my life hearing such. Knock in the night on our lonely door! Cold hand took hold of my heart, my children, and made fist. No reason for person to be outside with dark spirit walking. Who was out there now was on feet of cat, brought by leopard, and with no good news.

I WISHED AGAIN FOR LIGHT. I wished again that we had kerosene lamp like Auntie in town. I had many times begged Ma for such, but she always said it was dear and we would have to be always carrying kerosene out from town, and the distance was long, and now there was no man at our house to bring it. And anyway, she said, we did not need it, for no one read in our house again since she put up her Bible after Pa was killed.

Old Ma never liked Ma to read it anyway. Old Ma didn't like any book, but especially that book. She called it evil medicine, and even on the day she died, she spit when Auntie tried to read to her from it.

But I missed Ma reading. I once asked her why she stopped and she said it only brought confusion. She talked then about Monrovia and changes in the city and confusion, just how I talk about Kakata today. Africa is too confused, and it is because of book.

But in those days I thought I was too smart and nothing would do me but book. I begged Ma to let me go to school to learn book. Many many times I begged, but she always said no, until I begged away her patience. Then with the mission people also talking the matter so long to her for me, finally she agreed. And I first began to read! Ah, my man!

Then we began to buy kerosene, that which I carried, to have light to read by. And today at last we have current in the house. And so what?

Maybe I can find money to buy box. Then Smallboy can make small market selling cold drinks. I think he would like that, ain't it?

But this black night was before I learned book and before we had kerosene, when things were as they were and not as they are. Those days, when night came to this house we did not try to stop it.

Kpa! Kpa! Kpa!

I heard Ma get up and find her way over us in darkness to the door. Her foot brushed my arm as she went, and I reached out, too late, to hold her back. Old Ma spoke fast and low in warning.

"Hawah! Take time!"

Now Ma reached the door, but she did not open it. "Who there?" she called.

"Maima Kiawu." It was voice of young woman, and sounding somehow sweet in my ear, you know.

"Who are you, Maima Kiawu, and what you want?"

"I tired," young woman voice. "We coming from Monrovia and going to Golata. The baby tired and heavy and footroad too dark to follow again."

"Who there with you, Maima Kiawu?"

"Just myself, my ma, and my baby."

Old Ma again, low to Ma. "Why they didn't sleep in Kakata, Hawah? What they are doing on road at night, walking with devil?"

"Why you left Kakata," Ma called, "when you could see night coming-o?"

Silence. Then came different voice out of the night. Oh, my children, I covered my head for fear of its sound, old and dry, like snake sliding over dead leaves. "This our first time coming to Golata. Man told us we could reach before night, but trouble catch us on road."

Old Ma whispered, "What kind of trouble,

Hawah? And how they could see our house is here, from across river? Ain't the moon is dark tonight? Don't let them in."

"I beg you," young woman voice.

"I beg you, yah?" old dead voice.

"Don't, Hawah. Let them walk on."

"But it too far, Ma. It too black."

"Don't, Hawah. They trouble-o."

There came long quiet while Ma weighed the matter. Slowly into the quiet came sound of baby outside—first moan, then whine, then sharp crying, that which like knife cut through Meatta baby sleep and brought her awake into this night.

I thought to myself, "That baby sick!"

"Ma. Ma," Meatta whispered, that which was her only word.

But Ma's mind was full so, she did not hear her baby, and Meatta too began to cry. Baby outside heard its echo and cried harder. And so did Meatta too. And with time caught in the night between two babies crying, myself I shook and began to cry.

"Don't, Ma, don't!" I said.

Ma came to Meatta and hushed her and put hand on my shoulder to feel safe again. Woman outside talked low to her baby, but it stay cried.

"I beg you. The baby too tired. We only want to sleep here one night. We can't sleep outside for spirit. We not rogue. Please trust us, I beg you."

Ma moved to the door again. "There just you three?"

"Yes! Ain't I told you that already?"

Ma unlocked the door. I shook, expecting to hear noises of feet rushing, and waited for hands to grab me. But all I heard were people coming in, quiet. "Thank you, thank you." And all I felt was sweet cool air falling into our house where all the day heat was trapped. Then Ma locked the door again, and stale hot heavy air closed back on me. "Thank you, thank you."

"You hungry?" That Old Ma, getting up, mad-o!

"Yes." Young woman, Maima Kiawu, spoke. "But don't trouble. We brought food."

"I will stir up cookfire," Old Ma said, and started for the door.

"No," Maima Kiawu. "Food stay warm."

"Stay warm?" Old Ma suspicious.

"Yes, we cooked it in Kakata."

Old Ma jumped on it. "You left Kakata with food ready to eat? With night so close? And spirit coming to walk? Why?"

"Feed the baby," old dead voice snapped like dry stick. Then to Old Ma like cream, bad cream, "Man said if we came fast we could reach

Golata before dark. So we packed our food and came without eating."

"What man? He lied to you."

"Seem so."

"Ma, why you don't bring mats for them to sleep?" Ma said, quiet like chief talking peace, you know. And after time, Old Ma moved grumbling to do so.

"You were lucky to find us," Ma said to them as they ate. "The night is dangerous in bush with leopard so plenty."

"The night is dangerous all over Africa," Old Ma on low breath, "with rogue and bad people so plenty."

"But we be safe, self, for we be Christian," old woman dead voice. "That why we thank you and bless you."

"Hunh!" from Old Ma.

They finished eating now and we all stretched

out to sleep. But sleep could not catch me. In small house we almost touched, and I could smell sweat of day on their bodies to keep me awake. And noises coming from that baby also too, like witch cough.

Long minutes. Then from Old Ma, snore. Minutes. From Ma, breath, long and heavy. They sleeping as I lay scary. From stranger women, silence. Then, *ruff-ruff*. Stranger women moving together close.

Tsss tsss tsss. Whisper from Maima Kiawu.

Tsss tsss tsss. Dead whisper answer from old woman, that which I could not catch but the words ". . . before the sun . . . " and then whisper stopped.

I lay there small, listening, my eyes closed in blackness, and when I opened them it was morning.

SOMETHING WAS DIFFERENT this morning, and it took me time to tell what it was. Ma and Old Ma and Meatta stay on their mats asleep, but light was pale. I turned and saw the door was open, letting in gray morning sky. Sun would soon rise. Women were gone.

I saw dark thing in one corner and crawled to it, brushing by Meatta on my way and causing her to wake. I found the thing to be stranger baby.

Urb-urb. Meatta started with her baby noise, so I brought her to stranger baby and laid them side by side to play together and keep quiet, to allow Ma and Old Ma to catch all their sleep. When Meatta saw stranger baby, she hushed and looked with wide eyes at the thing. This was her only time seeing any baby from so close, though she had seen women with babies on their backs walking footroad to Kakata, and though she had seen herself in the small mirror Ma kept hanging on the wall. Now she laughed, reaching out to touch stranger baby like children will reach out to catch butterflies chasing before them on footroad. But stranger baby was not happy and began again to cry.

I heard Old Ma sigh, that same old sigh she made every morning before getting up to start her day, and I wondered what it was like to be old and to sigh each morning. Then Ma turned over, and her eyes opened to look at me. "Morning, Momo."

"Morning, Ma."

"Where the women?"

"I don't know."

"Ain't they said where they were going?"

"They gone when I woke."

"Hunh!" from Old Ma. Then she rolled over and got to her feet. "They can't say thank you?"

"They coming back again," I said, "because their baby stay here."

Ma got up, stretching broadly, and walked to the door, looking out. "They not at the river. I wonder where they gone?"

"Golata?" said I.

"Without the baby? Hunh!"

Old Ma groaned as she picked up her mat and rolled it. Then she went outside to stir up the fire which stay sleeping beneath the ashes. "Momo, bring water for rice, and collect the fish."

I carried the bucket to the river and filled it

with water, that which used to be too sweet here in cool mornings of dry season after sleeping all night. Yes, if you can believe such, one time we drank from this river. No, you don't drink so today because people too plenty now, and some use it for toilet. And now the Mandingos have come too, digging it for diamonds and bringing mud. They not bad people, Mandingos, but they travelers. They don't live here, so they don't care for the place, some of them. Time and time you may hear our good Christians abuse them, calling them heathen, because Mandingos be Moslem and believe somehow different. But then, what you say for good Christians like that?

But to my story. I filled the bucket with sweet river and collected the fish that Ma had caught the day before and strung through the gills to sleep the night in the river. I carried both back to Old Ma at the cookfire and watched as she killed and fell to cleaning the fish. Slimery fish and sharp knife and only Old Ma's blind eyes to guide her hands. But gut, clean, scrape. How she could able, would I always ask myself.

Inside the house I could hear stranger baby, where she was lying next to Meatta, crying crying crying. And like crying was disease, Meatta caught it too and fell to crying. Then stranger baby fell to choking small.

"What a pair for early so," Ma said, coming out to us. "They pretty, for true, but they can be loud-o!"

Old Ma, finishing fish and washing rice, said, "Those women best come soon. Baby hungry."

Ma laughed. "And I don't have enough milk in these breasts for two big babies so!" Ma had big breasts to hang to her navel, and I remember thinking there must be enough milk inside for ten big babies.

"Momo," Old Ma said, "go look in their pot

and see how much rice the women bring. I will put it here to warm for them."

I went inside and looked where the women had slept, but nothing was there. "Pot not here-o."

"Not there?"

"Nothing here-o."

Silence. I returned outside to see Ma turn now and come back from the river where she was going to take bath. Her face was pulled very tight. I looked to Old Ma, her face, too, turned up, pulled tight.

"Nothing? You sure?"

"Only baby, self," I said, going to fire to put back stick which had fallen out. Why Ma was so suddenly serious? And why Old Ma stay so over the fire, not moving while wood spilled freely out? "Nothing but baby is all they left."

Old Ma sniffed at the air. She looked to the

house. Her eyes were always closed in her blindness, nothing but two red slits showing between her lids, but now it was like she spied something. She said slowly, like measuring each word for length, "Hawah, what wrong with that baby?"

Ma was off and into house like rock from sling. She came back with stranger baby, holding it up to sun for better light while it waved arms with bawling. I did not understand what was happening, but I could tell by Ma's eyes as she looked the baby over, and I could tell by the look on Old Ma's face as she squatted waiting by the fire, that something bad was wrong. Then Ma lost her breath, and her face twisted. I moved closer to look myself at what she saw, but she grabbed the baby away.

"Stay back! Smallpox!"

Before breath was gone, Old Ma fell screaming to the ground. She threw her arms and legs about so that she thumped and thudded like fish will beat itself on dry land.

Smallboy, ain't you remember that woman acting so that time when they brought her child to her, drowned from the river? That was like Old Ma, screaming out for minutes and beating the earth while forest around us and rising sun stood watching. Ma stay like stone standing, and even stranger baby in her arms fell quiet to watch.

"Give it to me!" Old Ma screamed like leopard in the night. "Give it to me. I will leave it in bush for leopard. Or I will take it far down the river and give it to Mommy Water."

But Ma looked down at the baby who was beating its hand now against her breast, trying to find nipple for milk. "No," she said, shaking like with malaria fever. "No."

"What?"

"No."

Silence fell on us. Wind blew, stirring dust, dropping leaves loudly from trees.

"Why?" Old Ma finally said, hard and cold. "What you will do with it?"

"I don't know."

"Then give it to me!" Old Ma screamed again, reaching for stranger baby. "I know what to do with it, and so should you."

"We can't leave it to die."

"Then we will kill it and do it mercy."

"No," Ma said, turning her body to protect the baby from Old Ma's fingers.

"You be out of your head?" Old Ma cried. "Ain't you know what pox can do? Ain't you seen?"

Then she suddenly turned to me and grabbed me by my shoulders, and I wondered again at

27

how she could find me in her blindness. It was my first time looking close at her face so, and it seemed like I had never seen it before, to see all the damage.

"Listen to me, Momo, and tell your ma what I tell you. You see these blind eyes? Once they were good like your own. Pretty eyes, sharp eyes, but pox came and grew on them and emptied their water from them. You see these pits all over my face and body? Pox dug them. I had sores to burn and itch and eat me, every inch of my skin, pox."

She turned now back to Ma. "You be out of your head, Hawah? It pox!"

"Quick," Ma said. "Take Momo and Meatta from here. Take them in town to Musu."

"What you will do?"

"I will stay with this baby."

"Hunh!"

I looked at Old Ma, strong woman standing there, facing Ma. Her dry gray hair, that which stood uncombed around her bone face, looked like raw sheep wool. Muscles behind her eyelids moved like hand making fist, like she was trying to see again.

"Why?" she said finally.

I looked now to Ma. And my children, even as we sit here tonight, I can't lose the picture of her from my mind. Too beautiful, head high, standing straight and strong, baby to her breast. Beside her, all Africa seem small.

"Ma," she said, "you can never know. You never had book."

"Book!" Old Ma spit.

"Yes, spit for me. Pa sent me to school, Ma. You too. What you thought I would do there? I read, and learned. They made me different. I *am* different. From you, from Pa. I don't know right anymore, and wrong. I only know I can't kill this baby."

"Kill it before it kill you."

"I can't."

"If it be snake?"

"But it be baby. Only baby, small so, and poor and without guilt."

"Deadly like snake."

"Could I kill Meatta? Or Momo?"

"If you keep that baby, you *will* kill them."

And silence fell again on us like rock. Stranger baby stay pulling and punching on Ma's breast. Old Ma looked old as the earth. Shaking her head, she turned finally to trees and river and said, "I don't understand."

"I know." Two words fell from Ma like cotton will fall on the wind. River ran faster and bird sang louder. Then finally Ma turned to me and said, "Momo, be quick. Go put together clothes for you and Meatta. You going with Old Ma to stay with your auntie in Kakata. Be quick now."

Through all this confusion of shout and silence came something finally clear to me. I was going in town. It was longtime since I had been there, so I was too happy to be seeing my friends again. I ran to pack and was soon outside again because there was not much to bring. Old Ma sat on mortar, stay facing out over the river, and Ma stay standing, watching her and holding stranger baby to her breast.

Old Ma said, flat, "How I will get back from town?"

"You can stay there. I will manage alone. Have Musu bring Momo and Meatta every day as far as the river and we can talk over across. When this baby grow well, you can come home, all again."

Old Ma say, "Who will take care of *you* when pox catch *you*?"

No answer from Ma.

"No, Hawah. Musu can carry me back. I will take care of you. Pox finish his work on me, he can't catch me again. Momo, give me your hand. Let's go now."

As I led Old Ma across the monkey bridge, I looked back to wave goodbye to Ma, but she could not see me, for her hand was over her face and she was crying. Stranger baby stay in her arms.

"Be quick now," Old Ma said to me. "Day not be week."

ON THE TRIP TO TOWN, I took care of Old Ma and she took care of me, and we took care of Meatta, all two. Old Ma changed her angry heart with crossing the water. She told stories now, old ones and funny ones, and sang songs she knew from when she was a girl.

Time and time would she stop and say, "Smell that? Look now for vine growing low with big white flower."

Or if bird cried would she point after it and say, "See bird there with yellow and blue body and red mouth? It sing *tu-tu tu-tu*." Her eyes were only red slits, but her memory was sight.

When we reached the edge of town we could hear Auntie, though we could not yet see her. Because she had learned small book, she was big woman in town, and like so many big women, too fat. And loud-o. She was shouting to two smallboys how to use cutlass in clearing the grass from the house.

"You cut, cut, cut, swing, and cut. Hey, you! Swing, like so. Cut!"

When she saw us, her little mouth dropped open, then closed shut again with snap, like a child will do when telling lie.

"Ma, what news?"

"Nothing good-o," Old Ma said, giving old sigh.

"Where Hawah, Ma? Why you brought Momo and Meatta without Hawah?"

"Take time. Let me sit." Old Ma held out her hand and Auntie led her to chair. "What wrong, Musu? You jumping like fly in web."

"Nothing, Ma. Nothing wrong." But anyone could see, even smallboy like me, that not everything was right with Auntie. She rushed speaking. "Where Hawah? You say you bringing bad news?"

Old Ma told her whole story. Her anger came back all again, and she hissed like snake when she told of the women leaving the baby, and yelled like calving cow when she told of Ma choosing to keep it. Time she finish, half the town around us listening. Meatta grew scary at so many people and began to cry. People nearest looked at her, scary, too, then at me, and moved back from us.

"But why Hawah kept the baby?" Auntie said, her voice shaking like frog eggs, her eyes big like duck eggs. "Why she did not get rid of it?"

"Because of book, she said."

"I don't understand."

"Hunh! Join with me. But that what she said. Musu, carry me back now. I don't want to leave Hawah longtime alone."

"But I can't go there!" Auntie cried and took big step backward. "I mean . . . Ma, the place quarantine now. Everyone in Kakata know about those women. We drove them from town last night."

Old Ma had started to stand, but now she sat back down like someone pushed her. She spoke, slow with anger. "You drove them from town? To us? Ain't you saw which road they taking? Why someone did not come warn us?"

Auntie stood shifting her heaviness from foot to foot without answering. Then minister wife Mrs. Gbalee spoke up and Auntie looked at her with thanks. Mrs. Gbalee was maybe the biggest woman of all in Kakata, those days. She and Reverend had been to Europe and to States, self, and had even been to dinner at president's mansion in Monrovia.

"We were happy to be rid of them," Mrs Gbalee said to Old Ma, in that pretty way she could talk, you know. "We wanted them out of town, that's all. We didn't think for where they would go next."

Auntie looked begging to Old Ma, but of course Old Ma could not see it.

"Take me home, Musu."

"But if I go there, the people will not let me back in town! Farm is quarantine now!"

"Just take me as far as the river," Old Ma snapped like dog over meat. "You can leave me there. Hawah stay over across. You can leave. Hawah come then for me. You won't touch on pox. You won't break quarantine. Ain't that will be all right with you, Mrs. Reverend Gbalee sir?"

Mrs. Gbalee showed she did not like this

manner of Old Ma addressing her, but for respect to age, she made soft answer, "Yes, Old Ma, if Musu keep this side and Hawah stay over across, we all keep safe."

Unhappiness all over Auntie's face. But she agreed finally to go.

"Momo!" Old Ma called. In all these people she had lost track of me.

"Here am I."

"You and Meatta will stay with your auntie here in town. You help her. If she say you do something, you do it. And always show respect for her."

Then Old Ma and Auntie, she who looked always back, started off toward the farm, leaving me with Meatta in town.

I looked for my old friends, but was shy at first when I found them because I had not seen them for such longtime. They were kicking ball. Soon I was ready to join them. But just then the game got broken up by young woman who stumbled through, somehow funny. We all laughed because we could smell cane juice on her and knew she was drunk-o. Some of the children shouted at her and when she turned on them, then would they run and scream and everyone would laugh louder. She picked up rock to chunk one boy who was singing out, calling her Mommy Cane Juice, but she was too drunk for good aim. But her idea went now to the children, and soon all were chunking her back with small-small stones and sticks, stay laughing, even if it was not funny again. The woman caught hard time to stand before them.

Then the mothers came to see what was causing the noise, and when they saw the woman they began abusing her, but without laughing. One woman brought straw handbroom and laid it hard on the woman's back and head.

"Go from my child! Go!"

"Ain't we told you to stay from Kakata?"

The drunk woman looked around her afraid, and too confused, then ran out of town how she came, back toward Golata, falling time and time. But with women upon her, then would she get up and run again in fear.

The children went back to play, wrestling now, and I joined with them, leaving Meatta to play under orange tree. Soon I was playing hot and fast and all was warm with old friendship again. But then the women came back and pulled their children from the pile of legs and arms and bodies, leaving me lonely on the ground to watch them catch humbug.

"Ain't I told you to keep from them!"

"You!" one woman shouted at me. "You take your sister and go into your auntie's house. Don't come out again."

So I took Meatta inside and waited, wondering. Day suddenly seemed too long. The children were already playing again, Old Man Beggar, having fun, dancing, and making music, and asking money from who would stop to watch. And me and Meatta must sit lonely inside. Why?

Finally Auntie came back, but before she came inside, the woman who shouted at me stopped her, talking fast and waving her arms, her eye scary so. Auntie argued. More women came around them, all talking, and some pointing at the house. I was scary, thinking I did something too bad, and was ready to take Meatta and run for the farm, when the crowd broke and Auntie came out of it toward me, shaking her head.

"Momo," she said, "you can't stay here. People scary you have pox. I must take you back to your ma."

I was too glad, my children!

"Now! Go now!" the women shouted.

So we started off right then, me carrying Meatta. The women followed but kept distance between us, stay calling after us. When we passed by farms, men working there looked up and began to draw near to see what was causing the noise. Auntie walked faster. She kept far from Meatta and me and would not help with Meatta, so that I had to carry her the whole way, too tired. Even after women stopped following us, Auntie stay looking back toward town and talking to herself, like fat chicken, you know, and how when you chase it, it can't know which way to run.

It was late afternoon when we arrived at the river.

"Ma! Hawah!" Auntie cried.

Ma and Old Ma came running from behind the house, Old Ma carrying stranger baby.

"Momo! Meatta!" Ma laughed on seeing us, but then grew suddenly serious. "Musu, why you brought them here again?"

Auntie called, "People can't let them stay in town for fear the pox already caught them. Hawah, why you don't send that baby?"

Ma said something, but the sound did not reach across the water. Auntie waited small, then went on. "I will leave them here-o. I must go now unless night find me on road. I will come tomorrow, yah?"

And Auntie left. Ma crossed the monkey bridge, worry on her face, and took Meatta from me. She would never let me carry Meatta across the water, should I fall with her. I was glad to give her up, too weak now from carrying her. But when I reached up to take Ma's hand, she pulled away sharp.

"Momo, stay from me!" This was my first

time hearing my ma say such words to me. "After you cross, you must wash yourself and Meatta good. I know I must be covered with smallpox."

And that, my children, is when the bad times began.

So, Smallboy, you sleeping? Not yet? Bring us co-cola, yah? All will share, and so I will continue.

That night Ma put me and Meatta under one window, and around us she laid fire. First night I ever remember sleeping with shutter open. Old Ma was scary and argued so, saying spirit would surely come in and humbug us. But Ma said it was better to take chance on spirit than smallpox. We must have the window open to let out smoke and we must have fire to drive the pox from us. Spirit would not come where light was so plenty, and besides, Ma would stay there awake all night, self, to make sure spirit did not enter.

Now, myself, I began to be scary and could not sleep too longtime that night for fear spirit would come for me, sneaking and floating through open window, or that smallpox would come jumping over the fire to attack. I remember pictures in my mind of screaming thing like monkey but with claw and tooth, sharp so, coming for me and Meatta to dig out our face like on Old Ma. And with such thoughts, I fell into sleep.

Time and time that night when Ma would put more wood again on the fire, then would I wake with jump and cry, thinking smallpox had me. But then Ma would just smile at me, warm so, and I would lie back down. The fire burned bright, and smoke made my eyes to burn. One time I woke and found Ma sitting with stranger baby, that which was crying until Ma got it to take breast. Then Ma began singing, soft.

> This baby sick, she too sick
> And Momo and Meatta there
> And pox, he all around.
> Sick too sick.
> Pox, you can't see him.
> Pox, you can't feel him.
> Pox, you can't smell him.
> He float on air Momo breathe.
> He swim in water Meatta drink.
> Pox, where you are?
> Don't come here-o, don't come here-o.
> This baby sick, she too sick.

Then I began to come to know why everyone was so scary of this smallpox. How to fight him, when you can't find him? What to do?

And I went to sleep with new branded fear.

Next morning, Ma put me and Meatta into the river when sky stay gray. "Wash your sister good and use plenty soap. You must wash your face and hers three, four times." Ma washed too. She cleaned her breasts again and again, making too plenty suds floating down and away, then rinsed finally and began nursing Meatta.

"You see, Momo, with sick baby eating from same place, I must make too sure to clean it good to keep sickness from Meatta."

"Ma, why that baby bad?"

Ma turned from watching Meatta to look at me. When she moved, her breast slipped from Meatta's mouth, and she took time to put it back and pet her head. "That baby not bad. She sick. But soon she be well again, and then you will see how good she can be."

"But why people in town can hate her so?

They chased out her ma, and yesterday they chased out me and Meatta, self."

"They did not want to catch sick too. Just like I don't want you to catch sick, which is why today I coming to build new room for you and Meatta, to keep you from that sick baby. But when she well again, we will live together all again and have new sister. Let's see, we must think of name for her. Why not Seatta, sister to Meatta?"

"If baby sick, why not send it like Old Ma and Auntie say, and we keep safe?"

Ma looked at me one time, then her eyes went up to Old Cottonwood, tree that stay old when even Old Ma was smallgirl. You cannot find him now unless you go deep in the bush, but African cottonwood be biggest tree on earth, this one taller even than president's mansion in Monrovia. Old Cottonwood stood just over there, by the river. If you could put twenty men in circle around the tree, they could not join hands, he was wide so. At bottom, he stuck out knees to catch his balance, those which were covered with small forest of bushes growing out of Old Cottonwood like mold will grow out of bread. Among these bushes was one palm tree trying to be tall, but next to Old Pa Cottonwood it was just smallboy. Big white trunk went straight into the sky, distance of four houses set one on another, and then the first branches spread out from it, two brother branches level to the ground, each brother as big as a big tree. These biggest branches formed a cradle, that which dirt blew into, so that other plants grew up there like garden in the air, with ferns and vines dripping down Cottonwood's trunk. But no matter how far down they dripped or how far up the bush grew from the bottom, always the giant trunk stay showed, like long, strong white waist. Above the first big branches, distance of tall man farther up, came smaller brother branches running twin fingers out to beat at sky. And higher more brothers. I never saw the top of Old Cottonwood until the day they cut him down. He was good good friend but when they made footroad wide into motor road they were scary of Old Cottonwood and brought him down.

Now, as the wind blew around his branches, lifting the ferns, he gave out sigh, sounding like Old Ma in the morning. And Ma sighed with him.

"When you were baby smaller than this baby, self," she finally made answer to me, "you caught sick too. I didn't send you then, and I happy now I did not. Ain't you are happy too?"

Voice of Auntie from over across, "Hawah, what news?"

"Nothing strange-o," Ma called and then

laughed, because, you know, the news was all too strange, but such is the greeting. "The news too plenty, Musu, and all bad."

"I brought you rice and palm nuts. I will leave them here, and when I leave, you can cross for them. If there is anything I can do for you?"

"No, Musu, I don't think so. Oh, unless if you would care to bring us cooked food this afternoon. I be too busy today building small room to hold Momo and Meatta at night, for I must not keep them in house with sick baby."

"Oh yes!" Auntie cried, too excited in her face and voice. "I will surely bring food, but I will bring you something more than that again. Wait and see."

And she turned and ran for town, her fat body all over bouncing *boo-loop boo-loop*. Ma had to laugh at the picture, loud and good. And myself because it was too funny to see Auntie so.

"Why you are laughing?" Old Ma wanted to know.

"Oh, Ma, you missing your eyes today!" Ma said to her, wiping tears from her face. "That my first time seeing fat Musu run since when she was smallgirl. Ain't she was funny, Momo? Like cow in race. *Boo-loop, plop-plop.*"

Old Ma joined with us laughing. And the bush came to shake with it, the sound of it jumping in the trees, and the whole world looked good so that the pox wasn't even in memory, for that small time.

People from in town were very good that day. Men came before one hour was gone, carrying with them big sticks of trees, piussava, and palm leaves. They cut the ends of the big sticks to sharp point so we could easily beat them into the ground. And they split the piussava, that which is called bamboo by some people, into long thin sticks. They carried it all to the river, but would not bring it over across, so Old Ma and Ma and myself carried it over the monkey bridge and up to the house. Meantime, the men dug dirt, put water there, and made mud, that which they put in banana leaves for us to carry over across too. Then they left us finally and went back to their farms.

They did too plenty work for us that day, for true. If we ourself had to cut sticks and clean and point them, and bring piussava and thatch, and dig mud, the room would take too many days to build.

On our side of the river, we worked hard too. We beat the big sticks into the ground so that all were as tall as each other, distance of me on Ma's shoulders from ground. Put them in half-circle joining on the house but leaving gap for door. Took long strips of piussava to weave crossways around the big sticks, tying them on with rope, that which Old Ma wove from bark. Then we brought more big sticks again to put on top for roof, joining them with house roof and weaving piussava strips through them too. So now the skeleton for the room was there, with bones of walls and roof waiting for mud skin and thatch hair.

"This be man work," Ma said, breathing hard. "We don't know what we doing, and the thing will surely fall."

"When snake will bite, man will die," from Old Ma, "and we don't have man today."

"Come, let's rest," Ma said, "but not long. We must hurry to finish before sun go down. If we can manage."

While I rested, Ma fed the babies, and Old Ma, who was never quiet, made many trips to the river to carry back banana leaves of mud.

Then we all went to work again to chunk the mud between the big sticks and the sideways piussava strips. We worked long and hard. I did the low work because I was short. Old Ma did the middle, and Ma finished with top work because she was tall. I thought maybe my back would break, but just as sun started going red we finished, and I was still one boy with one back. The thatch we were only able to throw on top to cover for tonight and make straight tomorrow.

Now that we were finished, we looked at what we made, and it was ugly, for true. But there was just one woman with two babies to feed, one old blind woman, and one smallboy to build it. Myself, I was too proud and too happy to sleep inside the thing I myself built.

All during the day, Ma kept going to the two babies, one in the house and one in the shade outside. All two were crying every minute, and

Ma had to keep feeding them and washing her breasts, and feeding them again. Now we big people realized we were hungry too. Old Ma went to stir up the cookfire, looking too tired, when we heard noise over across. Auntie was there with three other women and bundles of banana leaves.

"Hey, Musu," Old Ma called. "The cow won the race?"

"You say what?" Auntie called back, and then, when she understood, opened in big white smile. "Not cow," she cried laughing, "just fat old heifer." And she did dance for us. *Boo-loop.* Then, with her three women, she put off quickly for town because it was coming to be dark, that which was no time to waste in the bush.

Ma crossed over and brought back with her the banana leaves, finding them full of food— rice, boiled chicken, palm butter, and greens. Oh, we ate that night, I tell you, my children!

IT WAS MAYBE FOUR, five days after this that Meatta started with fever. All day long, Ma or Old Ma was wiping her with wet cloth, sometimes wringing it over her to let the cool water run freely on her hot body, and then Meatta would shake and tremble and cry out. Old Ma and Ma took care of her but would not let me near. And although Ma said stranger baby, Seatta, was getting better, yet I couldn't go play with her either, too. So I wandered lonely.

Time and time people would come and shout over across for news. Usually they brought food with them. When Auntie came that day she brought can milk for the babies.

"I sent down to Monrovia for it," she called. "How the new baby?"

"Seatta getting better," Ma called, "but Meatta caught sick now."

"Oh no! Jesus God! Oh Jesus, no! Is it pox?"

"I don't know. I think maybe. Ma say it start so, with fever."

"Oh Jesus, have mercy! Ain't there is something to stop it while it stay young?"

"I don't know. Old Ma say only put cane juice on sores for to kill it, that which I been doing on Seatta. But on Meatta, it just fever and no sores yet."

And so they talked, until Auntie finally remembered smallboy me, saying, "Oh, Momo, look what I brought for you." She held up small ball and chunked it over across to me. "It came up from Monrovia, so it too fine. Now you play with it and stay from those babies."

That night I slept alone because they took

Meatta in with them. I did not sleep well. Time and time small room would grow so hot that I couldn't stand to have cover on me, then so cold again that cover failed to bring me any heat at all. And all night I was scary. Noises were too loud. Outside, if stick would snap, then would it cut through my sleep like cutlass. Then would mosquito sing in my ear to keep me from sleep, and when one would land on me, it was heavy like beetle so I would jump in fear. One time I wrenched my back jumping so, and the pain too bad that I began to cry and wish for day.

Finally I woke one time and could feel the morning. I got up to walk but found my legs weak like young rubber trees that can't hold up their weight of leaves in storm but bend to the ground. I went outside and walked around to the door of the house, like drunk man, stumbling.

"Ma. Ma," I called in whisper.

Then black circles started swimming behind my eyes, and I felt myself falling.

I can't remember much about days that followed, but they seemed somehow longer than years but shorter than minutes. They were filled with devils tearing at me and with Ma sitting beside me, smiling strong and warm to chase away the devils, sometimes for a while.

Then one day it was over. I can remember, though my eyes were closed, yet could I see light on them, coming and going and playing, like colored butterflies will chase themselves over footroad where bush is thick and sun is not used to shining. With the light there, devils now gone. I knew before I opened my eyes that it was morning and that I was by the water, that which I could hear running next to me. I opened my eyes and saw the branches of Old Pa Cottonwood stretched above, so strong again, and all his ferns and vines blowing, time and time allowing sun to touch my face, then covering him gently again like cotton clouds on bright day.

"You feeling good now, ain't it?"

I thought from her voice that it was Old Ma at my side, but when I turned I found it was Ma. She was looking just the same, stay smiling with eyes shining. But why her voice was sounding so old in my ear?

"You been too sick, but now you well again. Can you think how long you been sick?"

I shook my head because it did not seem I could make my voice talk from weakness.

"Six days. I found you at the door and your skin was burning with fever and you been sick six days. Now you must eat."

She fed me some rice with cassava-leaf soup, but it was hard to eat. Small-small can milk was all I could able. All the time she kept talking in that old-woman croak voice. I saw too now that her eyes were strange, like far away, like looking at me through water or glass, and dusty.

"Hawah," Auntie's voice came from over across. "What news?"

"Good news today-o. Momo fever broke."

"Oh, thank you Jesus!" And Auntie began with crying. "Oh, thank you, Lord. At least you left us this one child. Oh, thank you, merciful Jesus."

"Yes, this one be charm."

"Oh, Hawah, Hawah, why you didn't send that devil baby first day!" Auntie stay crying.

"Musu, I tired now. Don't bring that here again."

"How you could bring sickness that way to your family, and all for baby of stranger!"

"I beg you, yah. I too distress now. Tomorrow."

"But tell me how! To kill your baby, self, and Momo sick there?"

"They were open to it already, Musu. Pox slept with them one night already."

"But one night. Only one night, that which is not serious. I don't think pox caught them in only one night."

"But you don't know so."

"But I don't think so."

"But you don't know! And that morning Momo and Meatta, all two, played with Seatta. And with baby piss all around them on mat."

"I don't think . . ."

"But you don't know! How I would feel to sacrifice Seatta in bush to leopard for my family and then pox catch them anyway, in spite, from that first night? How I would feel to kill that baby for nothing?"

"But Hawah, that baby not your baby. That baby nothing to you. How you could take chance with your own baby like that? Tell me, how you can make it seem right in your head?" Auntie was begging now, not just asking, like she needed to know, to know to live.

"Look, Musu," Ma said, rising, and her voice rose too, like river in flood. "I don't know. I've talked the thing to myself, and talked it, and always the same answer, I don't know."

"But you must know!"

"I don't know! I don't know! I don't know!"

Ma tore my heart, screaming. She swayed on river edge like cobra standing, neck broad and strain, and spitting. I saw her eyes full of water and shining, and she stumbled like that drunk woman that day in Kakata with all the children humbugging her with stones, and I knew now Ma was very very sick. Her foot slipped on the wet bank and she went falling with cry down and into the water.

Old Ma was somewhere near and must have

been listening to her two daughters fight, for she came now, running. "Hawah! Hawah! Where you are?"

Ma was like dead woman in the water, the stream rushing over her and washing her down the river rocks to drown her. Mommy Water waiting-o.

Auntie stay screaming, "Ma! Come quick! Hawah is in the water! Come quick!"

"Where? Where?" Old Ma was lost, arms out, worrying up and down at the river edge, her hair wild around her wild face. "Help her, Musu. For your Jesus, for your Heaven, self, you must help."

I went crawling after Ma, now far from me down the river. To do what, small sick boy so? Black circles swam again behind my eyes, and that was all I knew.

BEFORE I OPENED MY EYES AGAIN, I felt something on my arms, eating and burning. Strong, bitter smell of something like piss. I snapped my eyes open and found Old Ma pouring cane juice on my arm, and I saw it all over one mess of sores, black and yellow and red. That was the burning, that terrible hot juice on those terrible sores.

"Don't!" I cried.

"So you wake, ain't it? And kicking. Good boy. Don't worry for this. It pox, but not serious on you again because you strong to it. These your only sores, and soon they be gone."

"Stop! It burn!" I tried to pull my arm away, but Old Ma held tight.

"Yes, I know. I know all about that. But that good burning by cane juice to kill pox. Look, see this baby?"

She held up Seatta, stranger baby, and first time since that first day I saw her up close. She had big red spots all over her small-small poor body, and on her arms stay sores, like on mine. Old Ma's fingers felt softly for the holes.

"You see these spots here? Everywhere you see spot, was there sore, just like on you, each one. You want these sores all over your body, too, like this poor child?"

"No!"

"Then don't bring me your fuss. We must put cane juice there to stop them. She will be ugly now, her long life. But she lived. I don't know how."

"Where Meatta?" I remembered how Meatta caught sick so long ago.

Old Ma did not answer straight. She looked at river. She looked at Old Pa Cottonwood. She looked at me. Then finally she said, "Spirit took her."

"You mean," I said, trying hard, you know, "you mean she dead? Meatta dead?"

"Yes. Your ma did all she could able."

"Where Ma!" I suddenly remembered Ma falling, and her face down under the water.

"Sleeping. Musu carried her from the river, but she too sick now, like you were, self. But she will get well again just like you, ain't it?"

"I want to see her."

"Not until you better, all two."

I began crying to think of losing Ma to small-pox like Meatta, she who was too small, yet already gone. "I don't want spirit to carry Ma. I need her here."

"Oh, don't worry for that one." Old Ma

laughed. "Spirit can't come for your ma, only people too old like your Old Pa, may he rest, and young like Meatta, poor baby soul. Spirit don't want your ma. She too tough."

Auntie came outside then. "Momo, you wake? Good boy. How you feeling now?"

"What you are doing this side, Auntie?"

"I came to take care of your ma and you and that stranger baby." She smiled with pride. "You don't think Old Ma could do it lonely, ain't it?"

"But you too scary to come here," I said. I remembered too well how she made me carry Meatta whole way from town, how she was like fat chicken on the road, nervous so, how she would keep herself over across, and mostly how she almost let Ma drown so as not to pull with pox.

"I wasn't scary!" she said, angry. "I wasn't

scary. But why come soon when your ma stay well to take care of you? Why take chance until it be matter of must?"

"Momo." Old Ma, hard voice. "It not for smallboy to say if man or woman be scary. And Musu, you *were* scary. No shame there. If Hawah be more scary, she be well today and Meatta living. Bring that other arm, Momo. Cane juice waiting."

NEXT WEEKS WALKED BY LIKE turtle in sand. Each day people from in town brought food and they would call, "What news?" Each day would Auntie or Old Ma call back. "Stranger baby almost well. Sores on Momo finish growing and coming to dry. Fever on Hawah stay high."

"Sores coming now on Hawah. Fever stay high."

"Can milk coming to finish. Send to my husband's brother in Monrovia and ask him for more. Fever stay high."

"Sores coming now to cover Hawah. But fever finally finish."

And from the house each day came cry from Ma. Old Ma said her fever much worse than my own and pox was covering her over, that which I was strong to it and kept the sores only on my arms. Each day I asked to see Ma, and each day they said no because we might encourage the pox on both of us. But when they were sure my own was finish, then would they let me see her.

My sores bothered me from sleep to sleep, and though Auntie always abused me for picking them, I could not leave them be. Time and time my arms would burn and itch from them so that all I could do was jump about, or run, or play ball and try hard to forget them. I thought I would soon be like that crazy boy we see in Kakata today, to dance and sing and never sit.

Smallpox the most wicked thing in the world, for true. If it be gone now, as they saying, gone from the world, then God be praised,

God who put it here in the beginning. But take time and see.

At last my sores grew small and hard and dry, and the itch and burn was not so bad again. Once when I went into river for bath, some grew soft with water and I pulled them off. Skin beneath was raw and red, but I was glad to be finish with the black scab. Soon all were gone, and except for the skin being too tender below, I felt as well as ever I felt.

One day when same old news was shouted over across, I asked again to see Ma. Old Ma and Auntie talked the matter and agreed it would be all right. Inside, darkness was soft and deep. I moved to Ma but could not see much of her in the dimness.

"Ma." I was too shy from such longtime.

"Momo." Her voice was as I remembered, soft now, not like Old Ma's again. But somehow strange, like she was talking with her mouth full of rice.

"What news?" she asked.

"Nothing strange-o," I said. I looked for her teeth to show white in the darkness but could not see them, or her eyes shining either.

"Old Ma say your sores finish, Momo. It must feel good, ain't it?"

"Oh yes, Ma! I had them all over my arms and the itch too bad! And when Old Ma put cane juice there to eat them, then would they burn so I hoped to die."

"I know."

"And at night, I could not sleep for itching. I didn't know where to keep my arms."

"I know. I know."

Then we fell quiet. I listened to her breathing and remembered how, when we killed goat one time, its breathing was heavy and full of air so, and whistle and sob. I wanted to take her hand but was too shy.

She said, "Smell bad in here, ain't it?"

"Like dead rat."

"Call your auntie for me."

I found Auntie outside and told her that Ma wanted her. She took deep breath, then went inside while I stay at the door.

"Musu," Ma's voice came from darkness. "I want to go outside. I want good air on me again, and sun."

"You think you strong to it?"

"I think so, but you must help me."

"Well. Here. Put this cloth around your shoulders so I don't touch on your skin."

I heard Auntie grunt and Ma moan. Then when I saw their two shadows coming toward me, I moved back to allow them out. They stopped just outside, and a spray of sunlight came through the trees to touch them.

My children, I cried on seeing my ma, never dreaming she could be so. Monster. All over running sores. Her face was swollen with scab until her eyes were closed shut with them. Her nose was hill of pus, her nostril holes blocked up with scab. Her hair was gone, eaten away by scab. There was nothing to her head but folding rot.

"The sun feel good. It feel pure on my skin." When she talked, black hole opened. Scab kissed scab, and those were her lips.

"I can't see. Eyes stay shut. Take me to the cottonwood, Musu."

They walked toward me, Ma blind and Auntie staring wide but without eyes. I backed away. I saw Ma's breasts and arms covered with the sores and, when she passed by me, I saw her back was even worse, raw from lying on it. She stumbled and I looked down at her feet below the cloth lappa around her waist and legs. Bad skin there too. Bad skin and scab everywhere.

When they reached the river under Old Cottonwood, Auntie put down her cloth and helped Ma to lie on it. I could see from Auntie's bald face that she didn't know until now how bad Ma was. Darkness inside had kept it secret from her, but sunlight now showed it for display.

"Hawah! Oh! Poor Hawah!" Auntie began to cry.

Old Ma moved down to us. "Don't cry, Musu. Pox not on *you*. How you feeling, Hawah? The air fine?"

"Too fine."

"How the itch?"

"It stay there. But the air cool on it, and too fine."

"Your lips, Hawah!" Auntie down on her knees.

"I did not tell you, Musu," said Old Ma.

"Her lips!" Auntie turned to Old Ma with crying.

"Scab growing into scab and I had to cut hole for breathing, morning and night," said Old Ma. "The air better here, Hawah?"

"Too fine, Ma."

"Momo, you here?" Old Ma held her head just so, listening for me. But I could not speak for seeing Ma so and thinking of Old Ma in darkness, with sharp knife. Old Ma reached out her arms blind for me, and I went into them. "Take time, my man," said Old Ma. "No mind, yah? Your ma be well again. She strong for can milk, that which is all she can able now, because all inside her mouth, all scab, too. But soon, she be like you, you will see."

Auntie stay on her knees beside Ma, now rocking, now sob, now covering her eyes and mouth with her hands. "Hawah, I did bad, bad thing to you. I did not know you were too sick as this. Oh, forgive, forgive me, forgive me."

River slowed. Wind stopped. And even Ma's breathing grew quiet.

Then Old Ma said finally, "What, Musu? What you did?"

Auntie turned her face from us, but stay covering it with her hands. "That woman!" she cried.

"What woman?" said Old Ma.

"Maima Kiawu."

"Oh, Musu!" breathed Old Ma. "What you did?"

"Maima Kiawu came in town with her ma and baby and wanted to stay at my house, saying they cousin to my husband in Monrovia. She said she came on moneybus to live now in Kakata. She too nice, and the baby too pretty.

Women from in town were there to welcome them, and while Maima Kiawu was cooking they played with the baby. But they found the pox. Then did they shout. Then did they scream. They went for their men to drive her from town.

"Maima Kiawu looked at me with crying. 'Where will I go?' she said. 'My poor baby,' she said. 'They drove us from Monrovia. Now will they drive us from here. Help us. I beg you. You must help us,' she said.

"What to do? People coming, men with big sticks. Old woman, she with her wicked voice, ran and brought my Bible from the table. 'Look at this book! You call yourself Christian and let us beg you without Christian help? Heathen! Pagan! Jesus spit on you!' And she spit at my feet.

"But I could not keep them at my house. Men

with sticks coming! But I could not let them go without Jesus, with night coming, to die in bush. All I could think was you, here on the farm. I told them how to find you, but I said to stay one night only. One night, then go.

"What to do? I did not know she would leave her baby so. I did not know you would keep it. I did not know you would catch sick so. Hawah, forgive me. I did not know."

Trees listened, river rested, all watching Auntie on her knees before Ma, sobbing. Ma was quiet. Water ran from scab on her eyes and trickled into cracks of her skin, down to her ears and to the back of her head, wetting her like mud. She shook with coughing and fluids, then rolled to her side to keep from choking. She put her hand to her face, and I saw her fingers web now, like duck, scab joining finger to finger, even to her thumb, and burying her silver ring.

"Musu," she said. "If I was well, I would kill you."

Auntie screamed, "I know! I know! And you should!"

"Take Momo from here, Musu," Old Ma said. "He be hearing too much. And you stay from here, too. Tomorrow and tomorrow be time for such talk."

Auntie got to her feet and held out her hand for me, that which I took without wanting it. And Old Ma turned to Ma.

"Hawah, I coming to put cane juice there. It will take your mind. You ready?"

As Auntie brought me away, I looked back once, hearing Ma cry out, and saw her body pull straight and hard as Old Ma poured from her bottle.

That afternoon, after Old Ma and Auntie took Ma back inside, I picked up Seatta and started for the river. Auntie came from the house and saw me.

"Momo, what you are doing?"

I began to run, but Auntie was too fast, catching me just as I reached the water and grabbing Seatta from me.

"What you were going to do with this baby?" I didn't answer. Auntie hit my mouth hard. "Ain't you heard me?"

"I coming to give it to spirit to leave Ma," I said, grabbing for Seatta again. But Auntie too strong for me, and soon I dropped my arms, shook, and fell to smallboy crying.

"Momo, Momo," Auntie said, putting her arm now around my head and holding me close to her. "Don't you worry for them spirit. They not going to take your ma. They for bush people, not civilized like you and me and your ma. If she be taken, it be Jesus and God, our Father, and if Jesus take her, she be too happy to go because Heaven too fine place."

"Hunh!" said I.

"You hush that hunh!" said Auntie and hit my mouth again. Then she grew shamed and gentle again and held up Seatta to me.

"This your new sister, Momo, and you must take care of her just how you took care of your old sister. Ain't you remember how you carried Meatta in town and back again? You would throw Meatta in river?"

"No."

"You hungry? Let's go eat, yah?"

MORE DAYS GONE. Every day now Ma came out to take air under Old Cottonwood. She looked like fallen tree you will find far back in bush, rot with years of worm and bug eating it, and black with years of wet fungus mold growing. And her lappa cloth around her, bright with flower and bird and butterfly, making the black blacker.

She would turn over and over, trying somehow to stop the itch and pain, but since her body was covered with it, which way to turn? Which way to lie, to sit, to stand, even if she could able? Her mouth stay sores inside and out, so she could not eat, only take can milk like baby. And every night when she went inside, she left the cloth sticking with raw pieces of bad flesh and scab.

Old Ma was always the one to wash these cloths, because pox and Old Ma already pulled. Auntie could go free then, she who passed all her time in the river washing her own self and pouring cane juice there on clean skin.

Finally all sores on Ma turned hard to scab, and I knew now she was going to get well. One day we were sitting with Ma beneath Old Cottonwood, Old Ma and me. I was taking care of Seatta and watching the vines and ferns above, and how, as we talked, they waved and laughed at us, showing their gladness at living so high off the strength of such good tree. Ma was speaking, and it was good to hear her voice coming strong again so.

"Ma," she said, "if your baby was sick as this baby was, what you would do?"

"I take care of it."

"If you thought it would die and if you scary pox catch you, too, then what?"

"I dig deep hole and leave her there."

"To die?"

"To die."

"Your own baby, self? You would have done so with me?"

"Yes, with you, self. Deep hole and put my heart there to die too."

"And Ma, if someone came to you that you never saw before and was sick with pox, what you would do?"

"I would take stick and drive her."

"You would send her to someone else to take care of?"

Old Ma spit on the ground. "No. Musu was too bad. I don't understand her. And I don't understand you, too."

Ma laughed, but fell to choking. She turned

on her side, and after choking stopped she laughed again and said, "Well, that be good, because I don't understand Musu, and I don't understand you, too."

"Hunh!"

"Well, Ma, I not going to say I sorry. I must do what I must do."

"Hunh!"

Ma turned to me then. "Confusion, Momo, ain't it?"

Then we heard Mrs. Gbalee, mission wife, calling from over across. "Hawah, how you are feeling?"

"Better always, Mrs. Gbalee."

"And you, Old Ma? You well?"

"Trying, Mrs. Gbalee."

"Where Musu?"

"Here am I," said Auntie, walking from the house like bird to sing. "What news Kakata?"

"Nothing strange-o," Mrs. Gbalee made answer. "But Hawah, we all missing you there. People asking, 'How Hawah can let pox work on her so?' Do you pray, Hawah?"

"I pray very often, Mrs. Gbalee."

"But my dear, you must have committed very bad sin for pox to hold you that way. Why you did not come to Reverend for advice and confession? You must thank God now that you getting well. God is mercy. He can forgive the greatest sins."

"I thankful to be living, Mrs. Gbalee."

"Look at Musu," Mrs. Gbalee went on. "She there all this time taking care of you, and pox all near her, yet never catching. Musu, your heart must be deep and good. God must love you. If I have your heart, I know I will always be happy and safe."

Auntie, she who was too pleased and fat, said, "I try, Sister Gbalee. I try."

Old woman came down footroad now from Golata way. I knew her dry face from seeing her stop time and time to look across at us. Then would she turn back toward Golata each time. She never said anything, and I think I was the only one ever to see her there. Now when she saw Mrs. Gbalee on her side of the river, she tried to turn back, but Mrs. Gbalee called to her, saying, "How far you going, old woman?"

"Golata." Old woman voice came to us like dry leaves on dry wind, and my blood ran like river water, rushing cold over rocks.

Old Ma was up and spitting. "I wondered when I would hear that voice again. What you want, devil?"

Like cat will purr, old woman said, "You have good ears to remember my voice."

"You hear snake once, you remember the sound. What you want, devil?"

"They tell me pox gone from here."

"May be," from Old Ma, "but I see disease stay walking in the world. What you want here, devil?"

"I finish waiting now. You have my grand-baby. Give her to me."

Silence of shock. Then from Old Ma, "You have no shame!"

"Where your daughter?" Ma said now, stay like stone, sitting hard and heavy.

"Golata. She sent me for my grandbaby."

"So she has shame but you have none!" Old Ma stay shrieking.

"I came for my grandbaby. Give her to me."

"This baby for us!" I cried, holding Seatta close. Ma put her arm around me and drew us, all two, soft to her side. Then, stay blind from scab on her eyes, she turned back to where old woman stood across the water.

"What you left here to die," she said, "is

dead. She buried just there. Bring shovel and take her. And take your own dead flesh from this place."

Old woman angry now and pointing crooked finger at Seatta. "There the baby I talking! That boy holding my grandbaby!"

Mrs. Gbalee looked the woman up and down. "Old woman, I remember you now. I saw you when you and your daughter first came in town. I saw your grandbaby then. I played with her. That baby there not your grandbaby."

"You lie!" Old woman was like cat in corner, swoll big and hissing. "If you do not give me that baby, I will bring police."

"My dear," Mrs. Gbalee said, "police chief is my brother and also there when my husband christened Seatta. I sure he will be happy to tell you. That baby for Hawah!"

"I will bring Monrovia police."

"Now listen, old barbarian, and understand!" Mrs. Gbalee now finally hard. "Every person in Kakata will witness against you. You take your daughter and leave today. Go from Kakata. Go from Golata, self. We know what you did, and we will drive you out like we did before."

Old woman lost, all at once helpless and crying big tear and shaking sob. "It hard, it too hard. Always drive me like animal. What I did to make God hate me so? Give me the child, I beg you. I all alone. I lied. My daughter gone-o. Maima dead from pox."

"Where she died?" Ma asked.

"There, somewhere in the bush, out there." She turned to the bush, shoulders sag.

"Like she left her daughter to die, so you left her."

"Maima was dying! How to help her? I just old woman, all lonely. Give me the child. Please give me my grandbaby."

"What you left," Ma said again, "is dead."

Old woman looked around to each of us, even to me. When her old eyes met Auntie, she began to beg, but Auntie looked away, shamed, and old woman dropped silent. She turned, stepped small, waited, then turned back to us.

"Where I will go?"

"Where you came from, devil!" Old Ma gave her no pity.

So she turned and passed toward Monrovia.

Ma finally got well, all her scab pulling off. But her left eye bust from pox. All the water ran from the eyeball, leaving it empty and like the two eyes of Old Ma, red slit. Yet better than Old Ma, Ma's right eye stay with her. And her hair grew back after the sores left. But her skin was changed forever, looking like dusty dirt motor road after first big drops of rain will fall, all over pit and pile. And her lips, scar.

One day not long after Ma got well, she took me and Seatta to Monrovia, where we went to market at Waterside. Smallpox pits now were red and big in her face, so that everyone turned to look as we passed.

Ma was buying seed when one Mandingo woman came up to her, she whose face could hardly hold itself together for her broad white smile dividing it. Her eyes shone with bright light as she put her fingers to Ma's face, and she shook her head but with smiling, and touched with tenderness each scar while Ma stood quiet, watching her. Mandingo woman looked in Ma's one good eye, deep even to her soul, and brought happy tears down her own face.

"Oh," she said, stay smiling. "Oh, you must give me your heart."

So you, Smallboy. Ain't I told you now? Come, all to bed. Let's sleep.

AFTERWORD

I'VE LOVED THIS TALE of terror and beauty since I first read it more than twenty years ago, and I have shared it with readers in schools and libraries: the drama of the plot, the simple poetry of the storytelling, the immediacy of the place, the people, and the plague that threatens them.

I started off writing an introduction for this new edition, but I changed it to an afterword when I realized I couldn't talk about the story without giving away the secrets of betrayal and grace, from that first knock at the door up to the very last page.

It's always fun to hear a scary tale in the dark about the dark. A stranger knocks at the door. Do you let her in? She's in trouble. Will she bring trouble? But this isn't your deliciously shivery horror tale with a cozy ending. The physical facts of smallpox are horrifying. Many of those who didn't die were left blind, scarred, and maimed. The disease has now been eradicated. No one even needs to be vaccinated against it anymore. But the storyteller remembers when he was a child, when the plague invaded his home. It's based on a true story, rooted in the facts of daily life in one home in a West African village. The writer heard it when he was working as a Peace Corps volunteer in Liberia. One night the mother of one of his students told him this story about herself.

Besides the horror of the disease, the reason the story is scary is that the characters are so real. There are heroes and villains, but they change all the time. The townspeople who drive away the strangers come back later to help the survivors build a home. What about the aunt who salved her conscience by shifting responsibility onto her sister? Does she find redemption? There's so much love in the story. But pain can breed hatred and revenge, even among the best people, and then you need someone to stop you before anger makes you blind.

For me the most electrifying moment is when the mother talks about how she has changed. "I don't know right anymore, and wrong. I only know I can't kill this baby," she tells her mother.

You rush through this story to find out what happens. Now the questions haunt you. What is right and wrong? What would you have done?

Hazel Rochman
Chicago, March 2004